My Uncle Foulpest

Teacher Trouble & Spooky Sleepover

TIMOTHY KNAPMAN

SIMON AND SCHUSTER

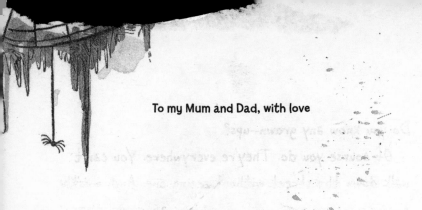

To my Mum and Dad, with love

First published in Great Britain in 2011
by Simon and Schuster UK Ltd,
a CBS company.

Text copyright © 2011 Timothy Knapman
Illustrations copyright © 2011 Sarah Horne

Simon & Schuster UK Ltd
1st Floor, 222 Gray's Inn Road, London WC1X 8HB

This book is a work of fiction. Names, characters, places and incidents are
either the product of the author's imagination or are used fictitiously.
Any resemblance to actual people living or dead,
events or locales is entirely coincidental.

A CIP catalogue record for this book is available from the British Library.

978-1-84738-937-4

1 3 5 7 9 10 8 6 4 2

Printed and bound in Great Britain

www.simonandschuster.co.uk

Do you know any grown-ups?

Of course you do. They're everywhere. You can't walk down the street without seeing one. And, mostly, they do a very good job. They look after us, they drive us around in cars and they cook us nice food. Sometimes, they even buy us presents and treats.

Grown-ups are all right.

Generally speaking.

But my grown-up is a bit different. He's my uncle and he's . . . well, you'll find out.

His name is Foulpest, which is strange enough, but the things he gets up to are so totally and completely weird and nutty that just thinking about them makes me go all red and wobbly.

So when I tell my stories, I like to pretend they all happened to someone else.

Don't get me wrong. I love my uncle. He has a good heart and he tries very hard, but he's just . . .

Well, he's just my uncle Foulpest.

Wally

TEACHER TROUBLE

It was Saturday morning. Wally was sitting in the kitchen, waiting for his breakfast, when the post arrived.

'I'll get it!' he cried. He jumped off his chair and ran to the front door.

He picked up the great wodge of letters that was lying on the doormat and started searching through it.

'Not for me, not for me, not for me...'

he mumbled, until at last he found what he was looking for. It was a postcard from his parents.

Wally's parents were very important people who worked for a very important company. They spent a lot of time flying around the world, buying very important things, and that's what they were doing now.

But Wally needed them to be home really soon. His school was having a parents' evening in two days time. His mum and dad would get to meet his teachers and see all the work he'd been doing. There would be a little show, and an art competition with a prize for the best picture of a sunset.

And this year, Mrs Dooper the head

teacher had said that the children could come along too.

Of course Wally wanted to go to parents' evening with his parents. But if they weren't home in time, he would have to go with...

No, he didn't even want to think about it.

So he read the postcard instead.

'Darling Wally,' it said, *'Look what we've bought! We'll just get it wrapped then we'll be home! Love Mum and Dad xxx'*

That was fantastic news! After all, how long could it take to wrap something? An elephant wouldn't take two days. Even if it was really bad-tempered and wouldn't stop wriggling.

Wally turned the postcard over and looked at the picture.

It was of an enormous bridge.

'Sydney Harbour Bridge,' said the words under the picture, 'is 134 metres high and 1,149 metres long.'

'*Blast!*' said Wally. An enormous bridge would take *years* to wrap. There was no way they'd be home in time for parents' evening.

So he would have to go with...

Oh no.

Wally thought really hard. There *must*

be someone else he could go with instead.

What about nice Mrs Beamish from next-door? Wally always went to her with his problems because she was friendly and kind and helpful and baked really wonderful fairy cakes. He'd love to go to parents' evening with her.

But Wally knew what she'd say if he asked her. She'd say he had to go with...

No. Oh dearie me, no!

But who else was there?

The postman!

That was it! Wally would ask the postman to go with him to parents' evening. He had a nice face. Actually, Wally had never seen the postman's face, but he had to have a nice face, didn't he?

There was only one way to find out. Wally opened the front door, but it was too late. The postman had gone.

There was nothing for it. He would just have to go to parents' evening with...

'Where are you, Wally boy?' It was his uncle, calling him from the kitchen. 'Breakfast's ready!'

Wally's heart sank.

'Coming,' he said glumly.

'Sit yourself down, lad,' said his uncle, who was rubbing his hands and smiling broadly. 'I've got a thumping great treat for you this morning.'

Wally's uncle, Foulpest, looked after him when his parents were away. He was kind and generous and good-hearted and Wally loved him very much, but there was a problem. A big one.

Foulpest was an ogre – a real one, with warts and great big pointy ears with hairs sticking out of them and everything. Foulpest tried his best to fit into the human world, Wally knew that, but he was big and clumsy and just a little bit revolting.

Anything he went near ended up getting sat on or squished or covered in goblin pong.

Imagine going to parents' evening with him. Wally went cold just thinking about it.

'I can't wait to see your face when you tastes this,' said Foulpest as he lugged his cooking bucket down off the stove.

Wally told himself not to be so horrible. Foulpest had been kind enough to make him breakfast and he should be proud to go with him to parents' evening.

'What is it, Uncle?' Wally asked politely.

'Porridge,' said Foulpest and he started to dish it out.

There you are, then. Foulpest had made him porridge. Something normal and ordinary and not at all yucky and disgusting. Everything was going to be fine.

Then Wally looked at it.

'But Uncle,' he said, 'this porridge is purple. And hairy.'

'Well of course it is, silly,' said Foulpest. 'It's purple hairy troll porridge. Made from only the finest hairs from out of a purple troll's nose. That's the treat. What are you waiting for? Tuck in!'

Wally didn't feel very hungry all of a sudden, but he didn't want to hurt Foulpest's feelings so he picked up his spoon. Then he froze.

'And Uncle,' he said, 'this porridge is moving about.'

'That's the goodness in it!' said Foulpest.

'That's the swarm of evil weevils in it!' said Wally. *'Yeuch!'*

He was right. A horde of mean-looking beetles bobbed up in the porridge and started swimming about as though they were on holiday.

'So *that's* where them little perishers have got to!' said Foulpest.

'Oi, you lot!' he roared at the evil weevils, 'I said you could sit in the porridge till you was warmed up but then you had to go. Get out of our breakfast at once!'

Foulpest rolled up his newspaper and thwacked away at the evil weevils but they were too fast for him and he kept missing. All he managed to do was send great globs of purple hairy troll porridge splattering all over everywhere until both their bowls were empty.

'Sorry about that, Wally,' said Foulpest.

Wally wasn't sorry at all. 'I think I'll just have toast,' he said.

Foulpest didn't *mean* to be strange. He just didn't understand normal, ordinary things like supermarkets and blowing your nose into a handkerchief and not letting evil weevils go on holiday in your breakfast.

And parents' evenings.

But Wally wanted to be normal and ordinary. He wanted to fit in and be just like everybody else. He liked his school and he liked his teacher, Miss Keen. He even liked old Super-Dooper, the head teacher. Oh, this parents' evening was going to be a disaster!

Wally took a deep breath and tried to calm down. He was being silly. He would go with Uncle Foulpest and that was that. After all, how bad could it be?

At that moment, Foulpest scratched his bottom and burped so loudly that the windows rattled.

Very bad indeed.

But there was no getting out of it.

'Of course I'll come with you to blooming

parents' evening, Wally boy!' said Foulpest, as he scraped purple hairy troll porridge off the walls and ate it.

'You know, it's a very normal school...' said Wally.

'I remember *my* school!' said Foulpest. 'The dinners was so nasty you had to eat them quick or they'd eat you!'

'...full of very normal people being taught very normal things,' continued Wally.

But Foulpest wasn't listening. 'They taught us Crashing and Bashing,' he chuckled. 'Smashing lessons was only for the really clever kids.'

'Well, they don't teach us anything like that at my school,' said Wally sternly. 'So when we go there we are going to be normal, all right?'

'Normal?' said Foulpest.

'*Normal,*' said Wally firmly.

'All right then,' said Foulpest. 'I will be normal.'

'Do you promise?' said Wally.

'Cross my heart and hope to die, smear your earwax on my tie,' said Foulpest. 'Now then, where's me tin of frogs' nostrils?'

'Why do you need a tin of frogs' nostrils?' asked Wally.

'I'm making scones for tea,' Foulpest smiled.

'Oh dear,' said Wally. He thought he might go and visit Mrs Beamish at teatime.

'Now, the first thing

about *being* normal is *looking* normal,' said Wally after breakfast. 'So we'll have to get you some normal person's clothes.'

'Say no more, Wally boy,' said Foulpest. 'I know just what you mean. Wait here.'

Foulpest stumped off up the stairs.

'I went to a Halloween party a few years back dressed as a normal person,' Foulpest called from the top of the stairs, 'and I've still got the costume. Frightened the living daylights out of everyone, it did!' Foulpest chuckled. 'Oh, sorry. No offence. But you normal people can look pretty scary to us poor ogres, you know!'

Foulpest came back downstairs.

'What do you think?'

Wally looked at him, his mouth wide open.

'I told you it was scary, didn't I?' said Foulpest delightedly.

It was scary all right.

Foulpest was wearing a big floppy hat covered in fruit, high-heeled shoes and a bright orange dress with frilly yellow bloomers underneath.

'You do realise that you're dressed as a normal *lady* person, not a normal *man* person, don't you?' said Wally.

'Am I?' said Foulpest and he looked at himself in the mirror. 'To be honest, Wally boy, I finds it very difficult to tell the difference. Oh, this is so uncomfortable!' Foulpest started wriggling. 'These bloomers keep disappearing up my bottom. But it'll be all right for parents' evening, won't it?'

'No!' said Wally.

'Can't I at least wear the fruity hat?' said Foulpest.

'No, you can*not!*' said Wally.

'Spoilsport,' said Foulpest.

They went up to Wally's parents' bedroom, to look through his dad's wardrobe. Wally's dad was several sizes smaller than Foulpest but

at least he was a man.

'Try this coat on,' said Wally.

'Oh, this is fantastic,' said Foulpest as he slid his arms into the sleeves. 'Nice colour, very smart. It must have cost a fortune...'

Riiiiip!

Foulpest was so huge that as he reached round to button the coat up, it split right down the back.

'Ah,' said Wally.

'Sorry,' said Foulpest.

'Don't worry,' said Wally. 'Dad's got a lot of coats.'

Which was just as well, because each time Foulpest tried on a coat –

Riiiiip! Riiiiiiiip!
Riiiiiiiiiiiiip!
They split right
down the back!

RIIIIP!

RiiiiiP!

RIiiiP!

Before long,
there was only one coat
left in the wardrobe.

'Just for a change,' said Wally, 'don't button this one up.'

'Whatever you say, Wally boy,' said Foulpest, putting the coat on very carefully. 'So this is what normal people look like, is it?'

'Yes,' said Wally.

'Only I can't really move me blooming arms because I'm scared of ripping the coat,' said Foulpest. 'So they're just sticking out sideways.'

'That's okay,' said Wally.

'Except that me nose is itching,' said Foulpest.

Wally scratched Foulpest's nose for him.

'Oh, thank you,' said Foulpest with some relief.

'Now, let's get these trousers on,' said

Wally. Then he looked at the trousers. They were far too small for Foulpest's tree-trunk legs and blancmange-wobbly tummy. But Foulpest *couldn't* go to parents' evening in just his bloomers.

'Ooh! Erp! Yeesh!' said Foulpest as Wally put the trousers on him.

'Breathe in!' said Wally, trying to do the trousers up.

'I *am* breathing in!' gasped Foulpest. *'Gnnnnrrrrr...'*

Foulpest's face went all sweaty. His cheeks flapped. His eyes boggled and crossed.

'Nearly there!' said Wally. 'That's it! Now, how do they feel?'

'Nggg!' said Foulpest. He'd gone a very funny colour.

Wally looked at Foulpest.

'I don't think we'll bother with a tie,' he said.

Foulpest opened his mouth to speak but no sound came out. He started shaking.

'What's the matter?' said Wally.

Foulpest twitched his nose.

'Do you want me to scratch your nose again?' asked Wally.

Foulpest shook his head.

'Are you hungry?'

'Ah – ' said Foulpest.

'Are you hot?' asked Wally.

'Ah – ' said Foulpest.

'Cold?' asked Wally.

'Ah – ' said Foulpest.

Wally went up really close to Foulpest.

'What is it, Uncle?' he said.

'Ah - ' said Foulpest. **'Ah - Ah -**
ATISHOOOOO!'

He sneezed so hard that the coat split down the back, the sleeves flew off, his trousers burst and Wally was sent flying across the room covered in green, custardy ogre snot.

'Sorry, Wally boy,' said Foulpest. 'I think I must be allergic to them trousers.'

Wally did nothing but worry for the rest of the weekend.

He was so busy worrying that he forgot to do something very important. He even forgot what it was that he'd forgotten to do!

And then it was after school on Monday, and time for the parents' evening.

'I'm looking forward to this,' said Foulpest with a big smile.

He was wearing bits of Dad's coats all stuck together with sticky tape and rubber bands. Wally had tied the sitting room rug round Foulpest's middle with a bit of rope. 'We'll tell people you're Scottish and it's a kilt,' Wally said. He had given up trying to find shoes that would fit his uncle, so Foulpest was wearing his own ogre gumboots.

'What are we waiting for?' said Foulpest.

Wally took one last look at him and said, 'Oh dear.'

Mrs Dooper was standing at the front gate, welcoming everyone to the parents' evening.

'Hello Mr and Mrs Cram, hello Bernard,' she said.

Bernard was always eating. He had his whole head jammed inside a jumbo bag of monster pizza crisps. He lifted it out just long enough to burp. *'Erk!'*

'Missed his second tea, bless him,' said Bernard's mother. She was vast and everything about her, from her hair to her toes, was grey. She looked like a battleship in shoes.

'Yes!' Bernard's father piped up. He was just as fat as his wife but absolutely tiny. He looked like a football in a suit. Wally looked at all the other parents queuing to get into the school. Some had pink spiky hair and rings through their noses, others had tattoos or wore crazy-coloured clothes. Compared to them, Foulpest actually looked quite normal - even if he did keep wriggling his bottom.

So, instead of screaming and running away (which is what Wally was expecting her to do), Mrs Dooper smiled and reached up to shake Foulpest's huge hand.

Maybe everything was going to be okay after all.

'This is my Uncle Foulpest,' said Wally.

'Of course,' said Mrs Dooper. 'How lovely to meet you. If you go into the hall, the show will be starting soon. Then you can explore the school, meet Wally's teachers and see some of the work he's been doing.

It's been smashing this term, hasn't it, Wally?'

'So you does teach Smashing then?' said Foulpest. 'See, I knew you was a clever kid, Wally.'

Then he wriggled again. 'Ooh, this rug's perishing itchy!' And he gave his bottom a great big scratch.

'Uncle Foulpest!' hissed Wally.

'Sorry,' said Foulpest. 'I mean this *kilt's* perishing itchy. I'm Scottish, you see.'

He winked at Mrs Dooper.

Mrs Dooper decided it was time to talk about something else.

'And at the end of the evening, we'll be judging the art competition,' she said. 'I can't wait to see your picture of a sunset, Wally.'

Wally went cold all over.

Of course! *That* was what he should have been doing this weekend: painting a picture of a sunset for the competition – but he'd been so busy worrying about Foulpest that he'd completely forgotten!

Wally didn't know what to say.

So he just went red and pushed Foulpest into the school.

As the children arrived, Miss Dash, who did art, was putting their pictures of sunsets up along the corridors.

'These are blooming amazing!' said Foulpest as Wally pushed him past them as fast as he could.

Looking at the pictures made Wally feel very guilty.

'That one there is wonderful!' Foulpest said. 'And, ooh, how about that one? How does you make them so colourful?'

'It's called "paint", Uncle,' said Wally.

'"Paint", eh?' said Foulpest. 'Well, it looks brilliant.'

'We wanted to fill our boring old corridors with colour,' said Miss Dash. 'That's why we asked everyone to make a picture of a sunset. I've been looking forward to seeing yours, Wally. I bet it's marvellous. Have you got it with you?'

'Thank you, Miss Dash,' said Wally, 'but erm... I'm afraid I've left it in my... Oh look, the show's about to start. I'll bring it later, Miss Dash.'

Wally pushed Foulpest into the hall.

In the hall, chairs had been set out in rows

and lots of mums and dads were sitting down, waiting for the show to begin.

Wally saw Sam, his best friend, sitting at the front with his mum and dad and baby sister.

Sam waved and smiled at Wally.

'Let's sit at the back,' Wally said.

'Don't you wants to be with your friends?' asked Foulpest.

'No, that's all right,' said Wally.

Wally wanted to be where no one could see them, in case Foulpest started scratching or picking or squeezing bits of himself. Not that it was ever easy to hide an ogre.

Just then, the teacher, Miss Nutkin, stepped out onto the stage and everyone clapped.

Miss Nutkin was tall and thin and wore a spangly fairy costume with tinfoil wings.

'Hello everyone,' she said. 'This term, we've been doing a special project on princess fairies, haven't we, children? And here are six of them to sing you a song.'

'Oh, I love princess fairies,' said Foulpest. 'Did I ever tell you the time I played football with one? She played dirty, she did! Always kicking my shins, she was, and trying to trip me up!

36

They make lovely dancers, mind.'

'Not now, Uncle,' whispered Wally. 'We're supposed to sit and watch quietly.'

Five smiling girls in fairy outfits skipped onto the stage, then Wally's friend Tommy clumped along after them with a face like thunder.

Tommy was a girl – her real name was Thomasina – but she was so brave and funny, and just a little bit scary, that Wally was glad she was his friend.

She was also dressed in a fairy outfit, but she obviously didn't want to be. She pulled at it and wriggled as if it was all scratchy – a bit like Foulpest in his rug, thought Wally.

Tinkly-winkly fairy music started and the other five girls did a little dance. Tommy just stood there and scowled. She didn't even pretend to join in when the rest of them sang their song.

'We are princess fairies,
We fly about all right,
You can tell we're fairies
For our wings are silver and bright!'

The mums and dads clapped. Foulpest was delighted.

'I told you they made good dancers!' he said. 'That was thumping brilliant.' He cheered and whistled and everyone turned round to look.

'Not so loud, Uncle Foulpest,' said Wally.

But Foulpest wasn't listening.

'Again, again!' he called out.

The princess fairy girls started their

song again and this time Foulpest got so excited, he joined in. He jumped to his feet and danced towards the stage. His feet thumped down the aisle so heavily that all the mums and dads bounced up and down in their seats as he passed.

'Uncle Foulpest!' cried Wally.

But it was too late. Before Wally could rush up and grab him, Foulpest had leapt onto the stage, grabbed Miss Nutkin and was whirling her around in a crazy dance.

'Ooh dear!' cried Miss Nutkin. 'Shall we just calm down a bit?'

She wasn't used to dancing with ogres and was scared Foulpest would squash her or eat her or stick her up his nose.

But Tommy was loving it. Her face had lit up and she was clapping along in time to the tune.

The mums and dads watching weren't
sure if this was part of the show, but they
joined in with the clapping, just in case.

Foulpest let go of Miss Nutkin and
stamped his feet in time to the clapping
and the tinkly-winkly music.

And that's when it happened.

Foulpest stamped his foot down so hard on the stage that one of the floorboards came loose. It was like a seesaw: as the end Foulpest stamped on went down, the other end went boinging up.

Unfortunately, Miss Nutkin was standing on the boinging end of the floorboard. She shot straight up in the air and into the

ceiling, where she got stuck.

All you could see poking out of the rafters were her bony bottom and her spindly legs, which were waggling madly.

'Help! Help!' she cried out.

'I'll get you down, Missy,' said Foulpest, and he reached up to grab her.

'No you will not!' snapped Wally and he dragged Foulpest off the stage before he could make things even worse.

'But everyone can see her bottom!' said Foulpest loudly.

'Ooh, no!' said Miss Nutkin, 'can they really?' And she blushed all over.

Wally pulled the cord so that the curtains swished closed. He pushed Foulpest out of the hall as fast as he could.

'That was brilliant, Wally,' said Sam as they passed him. 'I've never seen anything so funny!'

'Cheers, mate,' said Foulpest. 'What a nice lad!'

Wally shoved Foulpest out into the corridor so fast that they almost knocked Mrs Dooper over.

'Sorry!' said Wally.

'That's all right,' said Mrs Dooper. 'But where's your picture of a sunset, Wally? I can't see it up on the wall.'

'My picture?' said Wally nervously. 'No. You see, Mrs Dooper...'

But before he could say any more, they heard the sound of Miss Nutkin shrieking from the hall.

'What on earth is going on in there?' said Mrs Dooper.

'Ah, well,' said Foulpest, 'we were having a dance and she did ever so slightly get stuck in the ceiling with her bottom sticking out.'

'What?!' said Mrs Dooper and she ran into the hall.

'Quick!' said Wally. 'Let's get out of here before she comes back.' He dragged Foulpest along the corridor.

'Have you done one of these pictures, then?' said Foulpest as they passed all the paintings of sunsets.

'No I haven't!' said Wally. 'I should have done it at the weekend and I forgot.'

'Oh, that's a shame,' said Foulpest.

He was right. Wally loved painting pictures and he'd been secretly hoping that he would win the competition. There was no chance of that now.

The best he could hope for was to keep Foulpest out of mischief until it was time to go home.

'I know what,' Wally said, 'let's go and see Mr Webb.'

Mr Webb gave Wally extra help with his maths. He wouldn't be dressed up as a big spangly fairy. There was no way Foulpest could do anything embarrassing to him.

Was there?

'Wally's a bright lad and he tries hard,' Mr Webb told Foulpest as he showed him Wally's maths book. 'But he does find sums a bit hard to swallow. He just needs a little help,' Mr Webb winked at Foulpest, 'if you know what I mean.'

Foulpest winked back.

'I think I do,' he said.

Foulpest picked up Wally's maths book. And, before anyone could stop him, he popped it into his huge mouth.

It didn't even touch the sides!

'What are you doing?!' shrieked Mr Webb.

'Giving Wally some help,' said Foulpest. Only, because he had Wally's maths book in his mouth, it came out 'Gibbing Warry slum herlp.'

And he swallowed the book with a loud **'Gulp!'**

'There,' said Foulpest,

'I didn't find his sums hard to swallow – they've all gone!'

He stuck out his tongue. It looked like a large wet purple sock.

'Yeuch!' cried Mr Webb.

'You can't eat books!' said Wally.

'Oh, yes you can,' said Foulpest. 'I just did. Didn't you see me?'

'I mean, you *shouldn't* eat books!' said Wally.

'But I thought that's what you wanted me to do!' said Foulpest to Mr Webb.

'When I said Wally needed some help, I meant you should show him how to *do* his sums,' said Mr Webb. 'Not *eat* them!'

Foulpest laughed out loud.

'Me? Show Wally how to do his sums?' he roared. 'That's a good joke!'

Then he saw that Mr Webb was serious.

'Oh... sorry!' said Foulpest. 'Could you be a bit clearer next time? Right, I'll get the book back.'

And he started to put his finger down his throat.

'You are NOT going to sick that book back up again!' said Wally.

'You don't want to wait till it comes out the other end, do you?' said Foulpest, surprised. 'It might take a while.'

'No we do not!' cried Mr Webb and Wally in unison.

'But I thought you wanted it back!' said Foulpest. 'Make your minds up! Is there something wrong, Mr Webb?'

'No,' said Mr Webb, but he had gone a funny colour and looked like he was going to faint.

'Thank you very much, Mr Webb,' said Wally quickly. 'I think we'd better be going now.'

In the corridor outside, Foulpest said 'Nice feller. Now, who shall we go and see next? How about that Miss Keen you're always talking about?'

Wally thought about going to see his class teacher, Miss Keen, but he really liked her. He didn't want Foulpest doing something revolting in front of her.

Then he heard Mrs Dooper calling out, 'Wally, where are you? I'd like a word, please!'

'Wally boy,' said Foulpest thoughtfully, 'I ain't done nothing wrong, have I?'

'Of course not,' said Wally. 'Oh look, there's the art room! Quick, let's go and hide in the cupboard!'

Mrs Dooper had sounded rather cross.

'It's very dark in here,' said Foulpest. 'And there's not much room.'

'Shh!' said Wally.

'Sorry,' whispered Foulpest.

Nobody said anything for a moment, then Foulpest said, 'I think Mrs Dooper must have gone by now. I can't hear her voice any more. Why don't you want to see her, anyway?'

'You wouldn't understand,' said Wally.

'Oh, Wally,' said Foulpest, 'I *have* done something wrong, haven't I? But what? All I did was enjoy that perishing fairy show and try to help you with your sums.

I don't understands normal people.'

Wally sighed.

'You haven't done anything wrong, Uncle,' he said. 'You've done your best and that's all anyone can ask. Thank you for coming to

the parents' evening with me.'

'Then give us a hug, Wally boy, and let's go home,' said Foulpest.

'That's the best idea I've heard in ages,' said Wally, giving his uncle a friendly squeeze.

Then... 'Wally?' said Foulpest.

'Yes, Uncle?' said Wally.

'That paint stuff,' Foulpest went on, 'that you make pictures out of, what's it like? Cold and wet and kind of everywhere?'

'Oh, Uncle!' cried Wally. He flung open the doors of the art cupboard. When Foulpest had given him a hug, he must have knocked over the pile of paint tins in there. The paint had gone all over the place and Foulpest and Wally were covered in it!

'Oops,' said Foulpest. 'Sorry, Wally.'

'Let's just go,' said Wally. 'Before we do any more damage!'

But there was someone else in the art room.

'*There* you are, Wally.'

It was Miss Dash.

'I still haven't got your picture of a sunset.'

'No, Miss,' said Foulpest. 'He forgot.'

'Forgot? But that was your homework!' said Miss Dash.

'I know,' said Wally sadly. He hated the idea of not doing his homework.

'Oh my goodness!' said Miss Dash. 'What's happened to you two? You're covered in paint.'

'I'll explain tomorrow!' said Wally and he grabbed Foulpest and ran out of the art room.

'Mind out!' said Miss Dash. 'You'll get paint everywhere!'

'I didn't realise you had to be so fit to come to a parents' evening,' panted

Foulpest as they ran along the corridor.

Foulpest was so big and clumsy that he kept bumping into the walls and putting his hands out to stop himself falling over. Pretty soon he was exhausted, and said, 'I think I'll just sit down for a couple of ticks.'

'There's no time,' said Wally. 'Besides, look!'

The main entrance was at the end of the corridor in front of them.

'All right, then,' said Foulpest. 'But I'm going to have a good long sleep tomorrow.'

Foulpest put on a last spurt of energy to make it to the main entrance.

Just as they were about to reach it, Mrs Dooper stepped out in front of them.

'I've been looking for you two,' she said.

'Mrs Dooper,' said Foulpest, 'we have to go, but I've had a lovely time. Thank you for inviting me.'

He picked her up and gave her a great big hug.

'No!' said Wally. He pointed at Mrs Dooper. She was now covered in paint!

'Oh cripes!' said Foulpest. He tried to wipe the paint off Mrs Dooper, but all he managed to do was spread it around even more. 'Er, sorry. Must hurry.'

Foulpest and Wally ran.

'How are we going to get out now?' panted Foulpest.

'There's a back door,' Wally panted in reply.

They skidded round the corner and ran

straight into –

'Miss Keen!' said Wally.

'Wally,' said Miss Keen. 'You're not going, are you? I thought you were coming to see me for a chat.'

'We were,' said Foulpest. 'Wally was really looking forward to it too. You're his favourite teacher, you know. He talks about you all the time.'

'Foulpest!' cried Wally. He wasn't supposed to tell Miss Keen that she was his favourite teacher! Wally wanted to die of embarrassment.

'Oh, I should say: I'm his uncle, Foulpest. Pleased to meet you.'

'And I'm pleased to meet you, Uncle Foulpest,' said Miss Keen.

'I'd give you a big hug,' said Foulpest,

'only I've just done that to Mrs Dooper and got her all covered in this paint stuff. Things have been going a bit wrong this evening, you see. We thought we'd better leave before she catches us and gives us a right ticking off.'

'Sounds like a good plan,' said Miss Keen. Was Wally imagining things, or was she trying not to smile? 'But if Mrs Dooper wants to find you, all she has to do is follow the trail of paint you've made.'

'What?' said Wally.

He and Foulpest looked round behind them. They had left great big splodgy paint footprints all along the floor. The walls were splattered and streaked from where Foulpest had bumped into them. There was paint everywhere.

'WALLY!' roared Mrs Dooper as she came round the corner towards them. Miss Nutkin and Miss Dash were following her and they all looked very cross. 'What are you playing at?'

'He ruined my princess fairy dance!' said Miss Nutkin.

'He spilled all the paint in the art cupboard!' said Miss Dash.

'And now you've made a dreadful

mess of the corridors!' said Mrs Dooper. 'What did you think you were doing?'

'Um... Um...' Wally burbled. He'd never felt so terrible.

'I can explain,' said Foulpest.

'Can you?' said Mrs Dooper.

Foulpest took a deep breath, then he said, 'No, not really.'

'Well, I can,' said Miss Keen. 'Wally wasn't making a mess of the corridors. He was doing his painting of a sunset.'

'What?!' said Mrs Dooper, Miss Nutkin and Miss Dash all together.

'Well, look at it,' said Miss Keen.

The other teachers looked again at the streaks and splashes and smears of yellow, red and orange paint which Foulpest and Wally had covered the corridors with.

Come to think of it, they *did* look like a picture of a bright and brilliant sunset.

'Isn't it beautiful?' said Miss Keen.

'Well...' said Mrs Dooper. She wanted to argue but Miss Keen was right. It *was* beautiful. In fact, it was the best picture of a sunset she'd seen all day.

'And,' Miss Keen went on,

'you did say that you wanted to fill our boring old corridors with colour.'

No one was more surprised than Wally when he collected first prize in the art competition. Everyone cheered and asked him to say a few words.

'I'd just like to thank my Uncle Foulpest,'

said Wally. 'I couldn't have done it without him. Now, if you don't mind, we have to get home for a wash. We're *filthy!*'

'Uncle Foulpest?' said Wally as they were walking home.

'I made a bit of a mess of your parents' evening, didn't I?' said Foulpest. 'Sorry.'

'Don't be daft,' said Wally. 'I was just going to ask if you'd come with me to the parents' evening next year.'

'What if your mum and dad are around?' said Foulpest.

'Even if my mum and dad are around,' said Wally.

'I'd love to,' said Foulpest with a big smile. 'Hey, we could paint the *outside* of the school next year! Come on, give us a hug.'

'But you're still covered in paint!' said
Wally.

'So are you,' said Foulpest. 'Come here!'

And, laughing, he chased Wally all the
way home.

SPOOKY SLEEPOVER

'Hey, Wally!' said Sam, Wally's best friend.
'You know how much fun we have when you
come to my house for a sleepover?'

'Of course!' said Wally.

Sleepovers at Sam's were brilliant. His
house was lovely and tidy. His mum and
his dad were friendly and kind. His baby
sister Jane was really cute. Better still, she
was very small so she didn't want to join in

with their games.

As well as playing games, Sam and Wally watched TV and read comics. Then, late at night, when everyone else was asleep, they took torches and sneaked down to the kitchen for a midnight feast. They raided the cupboards and made delicious secret sandwiches with whatever they found.

Nothing had ever tasted as good as a secret sandwich midnight feast at Sam's house - especially after a week of Foulpest's toad bogey pasta.

'Well, I was just thinking...' said Sam.

He was going to ask Wally to another sleepover! Fantastic! Wally thought about all the games and toys and comics he'd take with him.

'I was just thinking how much fun it would be to have a sleepover at *your* house for a change,' said Sam.

Wally's heart sank.

If Wally's parents had been around, of course Wally would have asked Sam over at once.

But Wally's parents weren't around. They were abroad, doing something very important for their very important company.

So Wally was being looked after by his uncle, Foulpest. Foulpest was an ogre – a real one, with warts and great big pointy ears with hairs sticking out of them and everything. Foulpest made a mess wherever he went and Wally was worried that if Sam saw the state of his house, or tasted Foulpest's disgusting food, he'd be horrified and wouldn't want to be his friend any more.

'I'd love to have you for a sleepover but erm... ' said Wally, thinking quickly, 'the house is being painted at the moment.'

'Oh,' said Sam. 'That's okay. You can always come for a sleepover at my house instead.'

'Brilliant!' said Wally.

§o-o-o-o-§

But that wasn't the end of it.

On Monday, Sam asked Wally again if he could come for a sleepover at Wally's house.

He also asked him on Tuesday, on Wednesday and on Thursday.

Every time he asked, Wally had to think

of an excuse why not.

'Erm... the bathroom doesn't work...' he said, or 'The roof's being mended...' or 'We're getting new carpets...'

And every time, Sam said, 'That's okay.'

But on Friday, when Sam asked him again, Wally answered without thinking.

'You can't come for a sleepover,' he said, 'because there's a stinky socktopus loose in the house. If it sees you, it'll grab you with its tentacles and spray you all over with its stinky socktopus juice that smells like pongy socks. *Yeuch!*'

The funny thing was, this was the only excuse that was actually true! Foulpest had been planning to make stinky socktopus stew for tea but the stinky socktopus had escaped before he'd had a chance to put it in his cooking bucket.

The moment he said it, Wally knew it was a mistake.

'A stinky socktopus?' said Sam. 'There's no such thing! If you don't want me to come for a sleepover, you just have to say, you know. You don't have to make up a silly story.'

Sam started to walk away.

'No, come back!' said Wally. He didn't want to hurt Sam's feelings. 'I didn't mean it. It was a joke. Of course you can come to my house for a sleepover.'

'Really?' said Sam. 'When?'

'Erm... next Friday?' Wally said.

'Brilliant!' said Sam.

'What's brilliant?' said Tommy, who'd brought her pet rat Guzzle into school to show everyone.

'Wally's having a sleepover,' said Sam.

'Wicked!' said Tommy. 'Can I come?'

'Erm...' said Wally.

'Oh, go on,' said Tommy. 'I'll let you tickle Guzzle on the tummy.'

Tommy was a girl, but she was so brave and friendly, and just a little bit scary, that Wally had to say, 'Yes, of course you can come.'

What had he done?

Now his TWO best friends were going to come to his house and see what a mess Foulpest had made of it and how horrible his food was! By next weekend, he'd have NO friends left!

'Who's having a sleepover?' asked Bernard, who was eating his way through an entire packet of toffees. 'Can I come?'

'No you can't!' said Wally. Things were bad enough already. He didn't want horrible Bernard coming to his house and pointing and laughing at everything.

'I don't want to come anyway,' said Bernard, spraying the three friends with toffee dribble. 'Wally's uncle's a filthy old ogre and ogres eat children.'

'Are you scared then, Bernard?' said

Tommy. 'Because I'm not. I'm not scared of anything.'

'You *will* be scared,' said Bernard, 'when the ogre puts you in his cooking bucket and boils you up and that's the end of you. Ha!'

'That's not true!' cried Wally. Foulpest was in fact a very *friendly* ogre, and he didn't eat children so they were perfectly safe.

Wally wasn't worried about *that*.

He was worried about everything else.

'What's the matter, Wally boy?' asked Uncle Foulpest when Wally came home from school that afternoon.

'My best friends, Sam and Tommy, are

coming for a sleepover next Friday,' said Wally miserably.

'But that's good, ain't it?' said Foulpest.

'Is it?' said Wally. 'Just look at this place!'

Foulpest looked around. Since he'd come to take care of Wally, cobwebs had spread across the walls. Clumps of bats hung from the ceiling. And the air was thick with the horrid pong of the dragon earwax that was bubbling in his cooking bucket.

'You think it's a bit too perishing tidy, don't you?' said Foulpest.

'No, I do *not* think it's a bit too tidy!' said Wally. 'I think it's a *dump*, that's what I think! Oh, Foulpest,' said Wally. 'What am I going to do?'

'Don't worry, Wally boy,' said Foulpest. 'We can clean this place up.'

'Really?' said Wally.

'Of course we can!' said Foulpest.

'But there's so much to do!' said Wally. 'If we're going to get it finished by the time my friends come round, we'll have to start right now!'

'So let's start right thumping now!' said Foulpest, and then he thought for a minute. 'Only you'll have to tell me what to do. See, I ain't never tidied up before.'

Wally's mum and dad used to have a lady who came and cleaned once a week, but when Foulpest moved in, she took one look at the mess he'd made and ran screaming from the house.

She had kept all the cleaning things in the cupboard under the stairs.

'Here we are,' said Wally, opening up

the cupboard.

Foulpest was big and clumsy so Wally didn't want him doing anything dangerous where he might sit on things accidentally and squash them.

But even Foulpest couldn't do much damage with a feather duster.

Could he?

'Take this and dust in the sitting room, Foulpest,' Wally said. 'I'll put some water in this bucket and mop the kitchen floor. But remember to be careful.'

'Will do, boy,' said Foulpest.

Foulpest tried his best, but he was so big and strong and clumsy that in no time at all he'd knocked a vase over.

Crash! It smashed into tiny pieces on the floor.

The moment he heard the noise, Wally came rushing in.

'What are you doing, Foulpest?' Wally cried. 'Oh no! That vase was Mum's favourite!'

'Sorry, Wally,' said Foulpest.

'Why don't you do some polishing instead?' said Wally, with a sigh. He gave Foulpest a can of spray polish. 'Here. Squirt a bit of this on the table and rub it in with the duster until the table shines.'

'Really?' said Foulpest. 'A little squirt from this can will make the table shine? That's a perishing polishing miracle!'

Foulpest took the top off the spray can and peered at it. He pressed the button at the top and polish sprayed straight into his eyes.

'Ouch!' Foulpest roared. He put his hands

over his eyes and staggered backwards out of the sitting room.

'No!' cried Wally.

Foulpest went crashing through the kitchen door. He tripped over the mop and put his foot in the bucket of water.

'Argh!' he shrieked. 'What's happened to my blooming foot? It's caught in a trap!'

'Calm down, Foulpest!' cried Wally. 'You've got a bucket stuck on it, that's all.

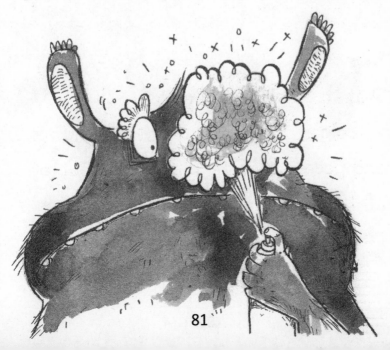

Stop moving and I'll try and get it off.'

Wally grabbed hold of the bucket.

'Now pull your leg back as hard as you can,' Wally said.

'Nrrrrrrr!' said Foulpest as he pulled and pulled his leg, until...

Pop! His foot shot out of the bucket. Water sprayed all over the kitchen and Foulpest went flying across the room so fast that he ended up with his bottom

stuck in the sink.

Squonk-Scronk-Slonk! went Foulpest's bottom as he tried to wriggle it out of the sink.

Wally decided that was the safest place for him and went upstairs to clean the bathroom.

Foulpest didn't believe in washing – and he'd certainly never had a bath – so he never went into the bathroom. That's why it was the cleanest room in the house. In no time, Wally had scrubbed the washbasin and the bath until they were both gleaming.

Then he lifted the lid of the toilet.

'Argh!' Wally shrieked.

The stinky socktopus was squatting in the toilet bowl!

So *that's* where it had been hiding all this time!

Before Wally could run away, the stinky socktopus reached out and grabbed him with its tentacles.

'Get off!' Wally cried, punching and thwacking at it. 'Foulpest! Help me!'

But Foulpest couldn't hear him.

He had finally managed to *squertch* and *squonk* his bottom out of the sink. He was desperate to make it up to Wally for causing such chaos, so he went back to the cupboard under the stairs. He saw the hoover in there and decided to do some vacuuming. After all, how difficult could that be? Unfortunately, Foulpest was so big and strong and clumsy that when he pressed the "on" button on the hoover, he pressed it so hard that the hoover started sucking at Maximum Super-Strength Overdrive Monster Suck.

At once, the hoover sucked pictures off the walls and carpet off the floor. It sucked up the kitchen table and the sitting room doors and even the gigantic sofa!

'Cripes!' cried Foulpest. 'Where's the perishing "off" switch?'

Meanwhile, Wally was fighting the stinky socktopus with all his might. He could see that it was just about to spray him with its pongy juice.

'Eurgh!' he cried, shutting his eyes.

And then something odd happened.

There was a terrible snapping noise and the bathroom door flew off its hinges and went tumbling downstairs. The toilet,

the washbasin and the bath were sucked down after it.

Then Wally could feel something sucking him and the stinky socktopus down too.

'Argh!' he cried as they both went flying through the air.

The stinky socktopus was so surprised that it let go of Wally without spraying him and disappeared into the hoover.

'What's happening?' cried Wally as he picked himself up off the floor and tried

to get his breath back.

'I think the stinky socktopus has jammed the hoover,' said Foulpest. 'It can't suck nothing in no more.'

'Well of course not!' said Wally. 'Look at the bag!'

The hoover bag was *enormous* – stretched tight and bulging.

'*Yesss,*' said Foulpest. 'Well, it has got half the perishing house in there. Tables, chairs, the TV...'

'But it isn't *nearly* big enough,' said Wally. 'Any minute now it's going to burst.'

And, at that exact moment, there was a terrible ripping noise and

the hoover bag
exploded, sending
everything it
had just sucked
up - the doors, the
cooker, the bookshelves -
shooting out in all directions.

The stinky socktopus went hurtling out
of the window, far above the town,
over the countryside and back
into the sea.

Wally and Foulpest looked
around them. The house
was now messier than ever!

'Sorry about that, Wally,'
said Uncle Foulpest.

'"Sorry"?' cried Wally.

'This place looks like a bomb's hit it! Now we'll never get it tidy before my friends come! Oh, this sleepover's going to be a disaster!'

Wally sat down. He felt like he was going to cry.

'No it ain't, Wally boy!' said Foulpest. 'I promise you that I can have this whole perishing house looking clean and tidy by next Friday. You and your friends are going to have the best blooming sleepover ever.'

'Really?' said Wally.

'Cross my heart and hope to die, eat your bogeys in a pie,' said Foulpest and he picked his nose and wiped it on the wall. 'One question, though.

BOGEYS

These friends of yours, they're not allergic to elves, are they?'

'What?' said Wally.

'Nuts, I mean!' said Foulpest quickly. 'They're not allergic to nuts, are they?'

Wally's heart sank.

That night, Wally had a very bad dream.

He dreamt that Tommy and Sam were both sucked into a gigantic stinky vacuum cleaner and that elves flushed them down the toilet.

It made him so anxious that next morning he popped in to see his neighbour, Mrs Beamish.

Mrs Beamish was always very kind and helpful, and she baked wonderful fairy cakes.

'Cheer up, Wally dear,' she said, as Wally helped himself to his third fairy cake in a row. 'Your Uncle Foulpest loves you very much. If he said that he'll have the house tidy by Friday, you should believe him.'

'I know,' said Wally.

'So promise me you won't worry,' said Mrs Beamish, patting his hand. 'Everything will be fine.'

'I promise,' said Wally.

'Come on, now,' said Mrs Beamish. 'I'll put the rest of these fairy cakes in a box and you can take them home with you.'

Wally tried to keep his promise, but it was no good.

He worried all week until Friday arrived.

On Friday, he worried all day until the bell rang for the end of school.

It didn't help that Sam and Tommy were both very excited.

'I am *sooo* looking forward to going to your house!' Sam said as they walked home through the park. He was practically bouncing along.

'Hey look!' said Tommy. 'A muddy puddle! Wicked! Who wants a big splash?'

'Don't!' said Wally.

'Why not?' asked Tommy.

Wally thought about it.

It wasn't like they could make his house any messier by walking through it in muddy shoes. Maybe if his friends were all muddy when they arrived, they wouldn't notice the horrible state of his house.

'Actually,' Wally said. 'I *would* like a big splash.'

And he and Tommy and Sam splashed through the big muddy puddle until they were all completely filthy.

When they finally got to Wally's house, Wally thought he ought to say something.

'Before you come in,' he said, as he turned the key and opened the front door, 'I just want to warn you that my house is a teensy bit un... *tidy?*'

Wally couldn't believe his eyes!

Instead of cobwebs, the walls gleamed with fresh paint. There were lights hanging from the ceiling, not bats. And instead of the horrid pong of bubbling dragon earwax, the air was full of the sweet smell of summer rose petals.

'Sorry, I think I've got the wrong house,' Wally said, backing out.

'But your key opened the lock!' laughed Sam.

Wally checked the number on the door.

It was his house all right.

Weird.

'Foulpest?' he called out. 'Are you there?'

Foulpest appeared from the kitchen. He was smiling and wearing Wally's mum's frilly apron. It was far too small for him – and it had flowers all over it!

'Hello, Wally boy! Nice to meet you, Sam and Tommy,' said Foulpest. 'Did you have a good day at school?'

'Who cares?' said Wally and he took Foulpest to one side. 'What have you done?' he asked.

'Just a bit of spring-cleaning,' said Foulpest. 'Looks thumping marvellous, don't it?'

'You're not... ill, are you?' whispered Wally.

'I never felt better in my life, Wally!' said Foulpest. 'Smell that lovely clean air! Yum! Mind you,'

Foulpest stopped and sniffed at Wally, *'you don't smell so fresh.'*

'No,' said Wally, going red. 'We played in a muddy puddle in the park.'

'It looks like it,' said Foulpest. 'Up to the bathroom and change, you lot, double-quick, while I put those mucky things in the washing machine. When you're ready I'll bring you up some drinks and biscuits.'

'What sort of drinks and biscuits?' asked Wally suspiciously.

'Lemonade and chocolate fingers, of course!' said Foulpest.

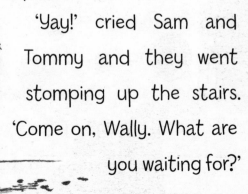

'Yay!' cried Sam and Tommy and they went stomping up the stairs. 'Come on, Wally. What are you waiting for?'

Wally took another look around the clean and tidy house and smiled.

'Thank you so much, Foulpest,' he said and he went stomping up after his friends.

Maybe this sleepover was going to work out all right after all.

They washed and changed into clean clothes then Wally and Sam dumped their bags on the landing. Tommy kept hold of hers and when the three of them went into Wally's bedroom, she put it down very carefully.

'Something special in there?' asked Sam.

Tommy didn't answer. Instead, she said 'Hey, look! Wally's got *Captain ZoomBox MegaRacing!* That's my favourite videogame. Let's play!'

As they were about to start, Wally heard voices coming from the landing. Strange, squeaky voices.

'Tut tut tut,' said the first voice. 'Muddy bags and footmarks everywhere!'

'They're nothing but a bunch of mucky pups!' said the second.

'Grrrrrr!' said the third.

Who was there?

Wally opened the door but when he looked out, there was no one on the landing. He was about to go back into his room when he noticed something.

Their bags had vanished.

'Here we are! Lemonade and chocolate fingers for hungry MegaRacers!' said Foulpest, coming up the stairs with a tray.

'Foulpest,' said Wally. 'What's happened to our bags? Sam and I left them here but they've vanished.'

'Making the place look untidy, were they?' asked Foulpest.

'I suppose so,' said Wally.

'Then it's not surprising, is it?' said Foulpest. 'Don't worry. I'll get them back for you.'

'And I could hear people talking,' said Wally, 'in funny, squeaky voices.'

'Funny, squeaky voices?' chuckled Foulpest. 'Are you sure you washed all the mud and mucky mushrooms out of your ears? I think you're imagining things, Wally boy. Here, cop this.'

He gave Wally the tray, pushed him back into his bedroom and closed the door behind him.

Wally was eating his biscuit when he heard Foulpest whispering on the other side of the door.

'Well, they want their perishing bags back, all right?' he was saying.

'But there was a terrible mess. Muddy bags and footmarks everywhere,' said one of the funny squeaky voices. 'I thought you

said you wanted this house to be tidy!'

Wally opened the door again but Foulpest was standing there all alone. He was holding their bags.

'Found them!' he said.

Before Wally could ask any more questions, Foulpest cried, 'Well, supper's not going to cook itself!' and disappeared down the stairs.

'Come on, Wally, are we playing *Captain ZoomBox MegaRacing* or not?' Tommy called out.

Wally looked around the landing but he couldn't see anything. Maybe Foulpest was right. Maybe he *was* imagining things.

The rest of the evening went like a dream.

There was pizza for supper – proper pizza too, like Mrs Beamish cooked, with tomato and cheese and ham on it, not Foulpest's usual pizza which was always half burnt and covered in frog spawn and tarantulas and roasted shark eyeballs.

Wally, Sam and Tommy watched TV and played *Captain ZoomBox* and read comics and then it was time for bed.

'Night, children,' said Foulpest, and he turned off the light. 'Sweet dreams.'

'Your Uncle Foulpest,' said Sam, 'he *is* an ogre, isn't he?'

'Yes,' said Wally.

'I mean, a *real* one, with warts and great big pointy ears with hairs sticking out of them and everything,' said Sam.

'That's right,' said Wally.

'But he doesn't do anything especially ogre-ish, does he?' said Tommy. 'I mean, apart from the way he looks, he's just like an ordinary person.'

'Do you really think so?' said Wally, delighted.

'Mmm,' said Tommy. Wally thought she sounded a bit disappointed. But he was so glad everything had gone well that he didn't think any more about it. He snuggled down and went to sleep.

Wally was woken by whispering.

At first he thought he must be imagining things again and tried to get back to sleep.

But the whispering wouldn't stop.

'Well, why did you bring him in the first place?'

It was Sam's voice.

'Because I thought it would be an adventure,' replied Tommy. 'I didn't *mean* to lose him!'

Wally turned on the light.

'What's going on?' he said.

Tommy and Sam were both out of bed. They'd got their dressing gowns on and were shining their torches under the furniture.

'Are you looking for something?' Wally asked.

'It's Guzzle,' said Tommy. 'I had him in my bag but he must have got out.'

'Your pet rat?' said Wally. 'What did you bring him for?'

'I thought he'd like it in an ogre's house,'

said Tommy. 'I thought it was going to be special, with cobwebs on the walls and bats on the ceiling and pongy smells and everything. I didn't think your house would be just like everybody else's.'

'He's not in this room,' said Sam. 'We'll have to search the rest of the house.'

'Quietly though,' said Wally. 'I don't want to wake Foulpest.'

Wally got his torch, and together the three friends sneaked out of his room.

They could hear Foulpest snoring. The noise was so deep and gentle and softly rumbling that it made all the furniture tremble slightly. It felt like the house itself was fast asleep all around them.

'Guzzle's a very greedy rat,' whispered Tommy. 'He's most likely gone to the kitchen to look for something to eat.'

'Let's check in there first, then,' whispered Wally.

It was so exciting to tiptoe through the dark house and down into the kitchen!

They closed the kitchen door and turned on the light.

'He could be anywhere,' said Tommy as she looked under the cooker.

'Maybe he's hiding in one of the cupboards,' said Sam.

'I know,' said Wally. 'Let's empty out all the food. That way he'll have nothing to hide behind. We can put it all on the kitchen table.'

As the table began to fill up with all sorts of packets and tins, Sam said, 'Hey, do you remember those secret sandwiches we made when you came for a sleepover at my house?'

'Oh yeah!' said Wally. 'Remember I had banana mousse and custard one night? It was scrummy!'

'Yes, and I had ice cream and chocolate cake!' said Sam.

'How did it taste?' said Tommy.

'Brilliant! I was nearly sick!' laughed Sam. 'In fact, while we're here, I think I'm going to have another one – with extra raspberry jam!'

Sam spread a piece of bread with jam and spooned ice cream from the freezer on top of it. He added a slice of chocolate cake and crammed another piece of bread down on top. Then he picked the whole thing up and took a great big bite.

'Great!' he chuckled. 'It's even messier than last time!'

'Shh!' said Wally. 'I can hear something.'

It was those strange, squeaky voices again. And they were coming from the cupboard under the sink.

'Tut tut tut,' said the first voice.

'It's nothing but a mucky pup!' said the second.

'Grrrrrr!' said the third.

'Who's that?' said Sam.

'You mean you can hear those voices too?' said Wally.

'Of course we can!' said Tommy.

'So I *wasn't* imagining things after all!' said Wally crossly. 'Just you wait till I see Foulpest in the morning!'

'All right, all right!' said Tommy, 'we're supposed to be looking for Guzzle!'

And she opened the cupboard.

Inside, were three little people. They were about a quarter of Wally's height and they wore spotless white overalls.

Their noses were all wrinkled up, as if they had just smelt a horrid pong, and they were scrubbing and brushing and washing and cleaning something.

Tommy shone her torch into the cupboard to see what it was.

'Guzzle!' she cried. 'You poor little thing!'

At the sound of Tommy's voice, the three little people looked round.

'Hey, you!' said Tommy. 'Leave Guzzle alone! What have you done to him?'

Guzzle's fur had been shampooed and plaited and tied with ribbons.

'That's better!' said the little people all together.

'Guzzle's a *boy* rat, you twits!' said Tommy. 'You've made him look ridiculous. Give him here this instant!'

But the little people weren't looking at her any more. They'd seen something far more interesting behind her. They all raised their arms and pointed.

'Tut tut tut,' said the first little person. 'Look at *him!*'

'He's nothing but a mucky pup!' said the second.

'Grrrrrr!' said the third.

Wally realised they were pointing at Sam. Sam was covered in jam and ice cream and chocolate cake from his secret sandwich.

'Get him!' cried the little people and, before anyone else could move, they ran out of the cupboard and surrounded Sam.

'There's only one thing to do with mucky pups!' cried the first little person.

'Scrub them till they're sparkling!' cried the second.

'Grrrrrr!' cried the third.

And they grabbed Sam and carried him over to the sink.

'Argh!' said Sam. 'Let go of me, you looneys! Help!'

Wally and Tommy, and even Guzzle, got hold of Sam and tried to pull him free, but

the little people were surprisingly strong.
They weren't going to let go until Sam was
completely clean.

'Uncle Foulpest!' cried Wally. 'Come
quickly! We need you!'

'Bloffle-ploffle-floffle!' cried Sam, as the
three little people turned on the taps
and started to scrub.

'Quickly!'

The door flew open and Foulpest burst in.

'What's all this, then?' he cried.

Goodness me, he looked a fright!

Foulpest couldn't find pyjamas big enough to fit him, so instead he put his feet through a bin liner bag and wore it like a huge nappy.

There were snails nestling in the spiky green hairs on his chest and he must have been eating when he nodded off because there was a slice of steak and kidney pie glued to his cheek with treacle.

'Oi, you lot! Stop that at once!' he roared.

The little people took no notice.

'Rotten little cleaning elves,' Foulpest explained. 'Once they've set their hearts on washing something, it takes a blooming avalanche to stop them. Hey, leave him alone, I said!'

And Foulpest grabbed the ketchup bottle and squirted ketchup at the elves.

'Well, come on then,' he said to Wally and Tommy, 'what are you waiting for? Give us a hand!'

Wally and Tommy picked up tubs and packets and bags and tins and threw

food at the cleaning elves until they were completely covered in it.

'Tut tut tut!' cried the first.

'Now *I'm* a mucky pup!' cried the second.

'Grrrrrr!' cried the third.

They all dropped Sam and started madly scrubbing away at themselves.

'I don't understand, Foulpest,' said Wally. 'What's going on?'

'Well, you wanted this place to be tidy for your friends, didn't you?' said Foulpest. 'But us ogres don't know nothing about being blooming tidy. It's not in our nature. I mean, look at me.'

Wally looked at Foulpest. The slice of steak and kidney pie fell off his cheek with a *schluuurp!*

'I suppose not,' said Wally.

'So I called in some cleaning elves,' sighed Foulpest. 'Sorry I pretended you was imagining things. I didn't want to spook you. And you've got to admit, they did a blinding job.'

'Well, never again!' said the first of the cleaning elves, still madly wiping himself.

'Oh, this is ground-in grime. We won't get
it out with scrubbing.
Our overalls will have
to be soaked! And we
had another job
to do tonight.
There's a boy called
Bernard and his house
is even messier than yours!'

'Really?' said Wally, Tommy and Sam.

'Oh, it's *disgusting!*' said the second. 'Sweet
wrappers everywhere and food stains up
the walls! Yeuch!'

'Grrrrrr!' said the third.

Wally, Tommy and Sam laughed.

'I don't know what's so funny,' said the first
of the cleaning elves, wrinkling his nose.

'You don't know Bernard!' laughed Tommy.

'We'll remember this, Foulpest,' said the second little person. 'And if you've ruined our overalls, we wish you a lifetime of greasy finger marks and stubborn stains!'

'Is that a promise?' said Foulpest. 'I like a stubborn stain. Cheers, lads!'

'Goodbye!'

With that, the three elves stuck their noses in the air and marched over Sam and out through the back door.

Wally and Tommy ran over to him.

'Sam!' cried Wally. 'Are you all right?'

'I've never been better!' said Sam, drying his face and smiling. 'What an adventure!'

'Really?' said Wally. 'But you were attacked by cleaning elves!'

'I know,' said Sam. 'It was brilliant!'

'And oh no, look at the house now!'

said Wally.

The cleaning elves had gone, taking their tidy magic with them. Cobwebs began to spread across the walls again. Bats flew in through the open back door and in no time the air was filled with the horrid pong of...

'Bubbling dragon earwax,' said Wally. 'It's absolutely...'

'Fantastic!' said Sam.

'Yeah!' said Tommy. 'Wicked!'

Even Guzzle wiggled his whiskers happily.

'What?' said Wally.

'This house!' said Sam. 'I mean, the cleaning elves were pretty good fun, but they made everything too tidy. Look at it now, though! It's a proper ogre's house at last! I love it!'

'Me too!' said Tommy.

'But your houses are lovely and tidy,' said Wally.

'Exactly,' said Sam. 'And that gets *sooo* boring after a while. It's why I wanted to have a sleepover here in the first place.'

'And best of all,' said Tommy, 'we got to see your uncle do some really ogre-ish things at last!'

'You want to see something *really* ogre-ish?' said Foulpest. 'Cop a load of this!'

He picked up Guzzle by the tail and raised him to his mouth.

'Hang about!' said Tommy. 'Don't eat him!'

'Don't worry, girl,' said Foulpest. 'I'm not going to eat him. I'm just going to set the little feller right.'

And he screwed up his face and did the

biggest burp any of them had ever heard
– all over little Guzzle!

As the horrid, pongy air blew over him,
Guzzle's fur stood on end and he giggled
away as if he was being tickled.

Foulpest smiled and handed him back
to Tommy.

'There. That's got rid of them ribbons

and plaits and the smell of that perishing shampoo,' he said. 'Only I can't bear to see a nice little ratty lad all scrubbed up like that.'

'Oh thank you, Foulpest!' said Tommy. 'He's all smelly and untidy again, just like he should be!'

'Though talking of food...' said Foulpest. 'You were making a secret sandwich, weren't you?'

'Yes,' said Sam.

'What was in it?' asked Foulpest.

'Ice cream, chocolate cake and jam,' said Sam.

'That must have been messy! I likes the sound of that,' said Foulpest. 'But I'm an ogre and us ogres like our food downright *disgusting!* Shall I show you?'

'Yes please!' cried Sam and Tommy.

'What do you think, Wally?' asked Foulpest. 'Can I?'

Wally remembered how scared he was that his friends would be revolted by Foulpest's messiness and his food, and now he could see that they loved it!

'Of course you can, Uncle Foulpest,' Wally said, smiling.

'All right, then,' Foulpest said. 'Watch closely. This is how an ogre makes a secret sandwich.'

Foulpest pulled out his food sack and rummaged around in it.

'First, we uses only the best beetle bogey bread,' he said, laying two slices of it on the table.

'Yeuch!' cried the children delightedly.

'Then we butters it with skeleton juice,'
he went on.

'Eurgh!'

'And we piles it high with banshee
blisters and piranha fish fingers and
any scab salad we've got left over from
Christmas,' Foulpest continued.

'Bleurgh!'

'Before sprinkling it with werewolf warts and – my favourite – zombie skin-leavings.' Foulpest grinned. 'There. It tastes as good as it looks, I can tell you!'

The children almost couldn't bear to watch as Foulpest lifted the gigantic sandwich to his mouth and took a massive bite. It went *everywhere*. Sam was sprayed with banshee blisters. Tommy was peppered with werewolf warts. Wally was covered in scab salad and skeleton juice.

And none of them had ever laughed so much.

'You know something, Wally?' said Sam when he'd managed to catch his breath. 'This is the best sleepover, *ever!* Thank you, Foulpest.'

'Yes,' said Wally. 'Thank you, Foulpest.'

'My pleasure, boy,' said Foulpest. 'Now, who fancies a bite of my sandwich?'

THE END